ACKNOWLE

For his grea

Jason Moser

maverickdesignworks.com

QUENTIN JAMES ADVENTURES:

QUENTIN JAMES and the UNDERCOVER AGENT

QUENTIN JAMES and the LOCH of ARTHUR

QUENTIN JAMES and the JACOBITE GOLD

QUENTIN JAMES and the GLOBAL WAR GAMES

CYBER SLEUTHS
Bug Wars/Zombie Wars
A Quentin James companion adventure

QUENTIN JAMES and the ARCTIC ADVENTURE
QUENTIN JAMES and the BATTLE for EDGEWATER
QUENTIN JAMES'S FIFTH YEAR at EDGEWATER

*

THE PRINCE OF LIGHT*:*
WITCHES" EYE
CASTLE ADVENTUROUS
THE QUEEN OF MAGIC

*

EBENEZER

*

THE LIBRARY
THE LIBRARY: Augustus.

*

THE O'BRIEN DETECTIVE AGENCY

*

UNREQUITED

Chapter One

'Eeewwwwww, Mum! Mrs Jenkins's cat has left another rat on our doorstep. Totally gross.'

'Don't touch it! Don't touch it! I'm coming, I'm coming.'

'As if I'd touch it,' said Tina, with a shudder.

'Bet Ben would,' said Lisa.

'Yeh, he's totally gross too. Remember, he ate a worm the other day?'

'Duh, I was there remember. That was funny.'

'Yeh, dare him and he will do anything.'

'Bit mean though.'

'He's always bugging us, so he deserves it.'

'Stand back, stand back,' said Mrs O'Brien, her rubber gloved hands held in front of her like a doctor about to start surgery on someone.

'It's ok, Mum, no need to freak out.'

'Freak out? Tina O'Brien! Where in the world are you picking up these words from?'

'School. I heard one of the boys say it at school. We shouldn't go, it's bad for us,' said Tina.

'Nice try, young lady. Have you done all your homework?'

'Yeh.'

'It's YES, there is an 'S' on the end, not yeh. Nice young ladies don't say yeh.'

'Yes, Mum,' said Lisa.

'Suck up,' said Tina.

'I am not,' said Lisa.

'Are.'

'Am not.'

'Are too.'

'Am not.'

'Girls, girls, go and play and be nice to your brother.'

'No way,' said Tina. 'Come on, let's play pop stars.'

'Yes!' said Lisa, as she tore after Tina who was already halfway up the stairs.

'Hello, Mrs Jenkins, how are you?' said Mrs O'Brien.

Lisa paused on the stairs to listen, fully expecting her Mum to tell Mrs Jenkins off about her cat, Twiddles.

'Oh, you know, getting by,' said Mrs Jenkins. 'Oh, has Twiddles been a naughty cat again? I'm so sorry, Jenny. I have no idea where he's finding all these rats. I trod on one the other day. It mashed up between my toes, horrible it was, all gooey.'

Lisa screwed her nose up as she imagined stepping on a dead rat. She shivered.

'What are you doing?' whispered Tina.

Lisa placed her finger to her lip, pointed to her ear, and then down towards the door.

Tina nodded and crept down the stairs next to Lisa.

'What are you doing?'

'Oh my god, you scared the life out of me,' said Tina, turning and slapping her brother, Ben.

'Muummmm! Tina hit me,' he instantly yelled, tears filling his eyes.

'Ohhh, you're such a baby.'

'I'm not a baby,' said Ben loudly.

'Kids, upstairs with you. Tina, I will be up in a minute to have a word with you. Can't you see I am talking with Mrs Jenkins?'

'Hello, Mrs Jenkins,' said Ben.

'Hello, Ben,' said Mrs Jenkins. 'Such a sweet boy,' she added. 'Such an angelic face.'

'Come on,' said Tina to Lisa, pulling her by her T-shirt. 'Baby,' she said under her breath, as she passed Ben.

Lisa looked at Ben, her heart ached just a little as Ben's eyes were so large and hopeful, filled with tears.

'Can I come too?'

'No!' said Tina immediately. 'We're playing pop stars, and that's for girls only.'

Lisa followed Tina into their bedroom, Tina closing the door behind them.

'We should play with him *sometimes*,' said Lisa.

'Why? He's a boy. No boys allowed. That's the rule.'

'Whose rule?'

'Don't ask me. I didn't make it. The world's rules I guess.'

'Oh,' said Lisa. 'What do you want to sing?'

Tina picked up the microphone.

Soon the screeching and shrieking sounds of their singing filled the house.

Chapter Two

REWARD

TWIDDLES
GINGER TABBY
Mrs Jenkins beloved cat has gone
missing, possibly trapped. If you
see her please call day or night.
01234 654 987

'Did you read this?'

'What's that dear?'

'Mrs Jenkins has these all over the village. Looks like Twiddles has gone missing.'

'Oh no, she loves that cat.'

Lisa slipped off her chair and went over to her Dad.

'Can I see?'

'Sure, honey, here.'

Lisa took the flyer back to the table, chewing her bottom lip as she read it.

'Tina, look,' she said quietly.

Tina shrugged.

'So what?'

'If we could find the cat, we would get £5. Mrs Jenkins is offering a reward.'

'Five pounds! Wow, we could buy loads with that.'

'We can talk to Mrs Jenkins about when she last saw the cat and stuff, work out the clues. I bet we could find her.'

'Ohhhhh yes, just like detectives,' said Tina.

'Yes!' said Lisa excitedly. 'We will need badges and I.D. cards, just like real detectives.'

'We could make those easy. I'll get the card, you get the colored pens.'

Lisa slid off her chair and dashed upstairs.

Five minutes later, they were sitting at the table, hard at work.

'What are you kids up to?' asked Dad.

'We're making I.D. cards,' said Tina, without looking up, her tongue between her teeth as she carefully drew a straight line.

'Then you will need a photo,' said Dad. 'I'll get the camera.'

Tina and Lisa looked at each other.

'At least they can't make us pose together,' said Lisa.

'True. And we do need a picture for the I.D. cards,' said Tina. 'So we can allow it. This one time.'

'Just this one time,' said Lisa, 'or they will want photos, like, everyday or something.'

'Tell me about it,' said Tina. 'And try and dress us in the same clothes again.'

Lisa gave a firm nod.

'What are you doing?' asked Ben.

'Nothing, go away.'

'Oh please. Let me play. You never let me play.'

'That's because you're a kid and we're nearly grown-ups now,' said Tina.

'You're not,' said Ben, crossing his arms. 'You're kids, just like me.'

'We're nearly eleven,' said Lisa. 'That's nearly a teenager.'

'I'm almost six,' said Ben.

'Hey hey, what's going on?' asked Dad.

'Nothing,' said Tina. 'Where should we stand?'

'Over here, against this wall,' said Dad.

Lisa watched Ben stomp away and sit on the sofa, arms folded, eyes fixed on the TV, though he glanced over frequently to watch what they were doing.

'Lisa, Lisa! Your turn.'

Lisa stood against the wall and looked directly at the camera.

'Smile, honey,' said Dad.

Lisa shook her head.

'Come on, honey, you look so cute when you smile.'

'We're not trying to look cute, Dad,' said Lisa. 'This is serious business.'

'Oh ok,' said Dad. 'Give me a mean face.'

Lisa frowned and firmed her lips and stared hard.

'Done,' said Dad. 'Give me a minute and I will print them out for you. Ben, you got a minute?'

'Coming.'

Lisa watched as Ben ran out of the room after Dad, smiling as his face switched from grumpy and stubborn to beaming and happy in an instant.

'Come on,' said Tina. 'Let's finish making our I.D. Cards, then we need to make a badge.'

'Already got that covered,' said Lisa. 'Come on, I'll show you.'

Together they ran up the stairs to their bedroom.

'Wait,' said Tina. 'I made this.'

Lisa watched as Tina stuck a poster on their door.

'That's not how you spell allowed, silly,' said Lisa, taking the black marker pen.

THE
O'BRIEN
DETECTIVE
AGENCY
No BROtHERS
~~aLOUD~~
allowed

Chapter Three

'Come on,' said Lisa.

Lisa pushed open the door and ran over to the trunk under the window.

'It's in here somewhere.'

Lisa pulled out the clothes they used for dress-up throwing them behind her as she searched.

'Huh ah,' she cried triumphantly, holding up a brown waistcoat with a silver badge on it. 'Our cowgirl outfits.'

'Great idea, where's mine?'

Lisa rummaged in the chest for a bit longer; a few more clothes joining the pile strewn all over the floor before she held her hand aloft.

'Got it.'

Lisa pulled the badge off hers easily.

'It won't come off,' said Tina, as she pulled and tugged at the badge fastened to her cowgirl vest. 'It's sewn on tight.'

'Come on,' said Lisa, and led the way to the bathroom.

'We're not supposed to touch those,' said Tina, as Lisa took the scissors from the drawer.

'That's when we were babies,' said Lisa. 'Now we're grown up we know better than to run with scissors, so it's all right.'

Lisa carefully snipped at the cotton holding the badge to the vest.

'There, done,' she said, putting the scissors back in the drawer. 'Best not mention it to Mum though. You know how over protective she can be.'

Tina nodded.

They went back downstairs to find their pictures neatly cut out and ready to paste onto their I.D cards.

'You need a name,' said Dad, 'for your Detective Agency.'

'We have one, The O'Brien Detective Agency,' said Tina, reaching for the black pen and carefully writing it atop her card.

'So, you are now officially detectives,' said Dad. 'With your first case, am I right?'

Lisa and Tina nodded. 'We are investigating the disappearance of Twiddles the cat.'

'Well, one good thing about her being missing,' said Mum, walking out of the kitchen, drying her hands on a tea towel. 'No more nasty dead rats on my doorstep.'

Lisa and Tina looked at each other.

'Hold up,' said Dad laughing. 'They're doing that twin thing again.'

Lisa and Tina turned as one and looked at their Dad.

'Twin thing?'

'Sure, the way you two talk to each other without saying anything.'

'Oh, right,' said Lisa. 'We don't really talk; we just know what each other's thinking.'

'Which is?'

'Rats,' said Tina. 'We don't like rats.'

'Ben; how would you like to be a Detective?' asked Lisa.

Ben looked over, his smile huge, his blue eyes shining.

'Can I, really?'

He came running over.

'You will need an I.D. Card,' said Tina. 'And you work for us. We're in charge.'

Ben's face took on a stubborn look.

'I'd take it, kiddo,' said Dad.

Ben's face instantly switched back to the smiling angel.

'You two can be Detective Inspectors, and Ben here can be a Detective Sergeant,' Dad said.

Lisa and Tina looked at each other before nodding.

'That works,' said Tina, 'as long as he knows he works for us.'

'He knows,' said Dad, with a sigh.

Lisa knew the warning signs and quickly changed the subject.

'You will need an I.D Card,' she said.

'I've got one,' said Ben, pulling out a black wallet. 'See.'

He flipped it open.

Lisa saw the shiny sheriffs badge first, then the I.D. card behind the clear plastic. Ben's "serious" face looking back. The O'Brien Detective Agency blazed across the top in red.

'Dad made it.'

Lisa was instantly jealous and tears pricked her eyes.

'Don't worry, I've got wallets for both of you too,' said Dad.

'Where?' said Lisa, her heart leaping in delight.

'Here, here,' Dad said, handing them both a wallet.

Lisa opened hers to see an I.D Card, all nicely printed with The O'Brien Detective Agency across top and her picture below.

'If you have badges, I can fix them in for you,' offered Dad.

'We do,' said Tina, holding hers aloft.

Within a blink of an eye, both girls were flipping their wallets open, flashing their badges.

'Detective Inspector Tina O'Brien,' said Tina.

'Detective Inspector Lisa O'Brien,' said Lisa.

'Detective Sergeant Ben O'Brien,' said Ben.

Chapter Four

'All the bikes stolen, can you believe that? Fancy coming back from your holidays to find your shop robbed. Hello, sweetie, are you poorly?'

Ben nodded.

The school nurse placed her hand on his forehead and then pressed her fingers against the sides of his neck.

'Temperature is a little high,' said the nurse. 'But his glands are fine.'

'I'll call his Mum to come and pick him up.'

'His sisters are in year six, might as well get them out of class and their Mum can take them all home at the same time.'

The nurse nodded.

The receptionist left her desk and made her way to the twins' classroom.

*

Lisa looked up as Mrs Sutton knocked on the door and entered the classroom.

'Excuse me, Mr Jacobs, could I take the O'Brien twins out a little early today. Their brother is poorly and their Mum is on the way to collect him.'

'Of course, Mrs Sutton. Lisa, Tina, please pack up your things quietly, and go with Mrs Sutton, and give your brother my best wishes for a speedy recovery.'

'Yes, Mr Jacobs,' said Lisa, putting her books and pencil case into her bag.

She caught up with Tina at the door and together they followed Mrs Sutton along the corridor to the nurse's office, which was right by Reception and the main entrance.

'Are you feeling ill?' asked Lisa, sitting down next to her brother and putting her arm around him.

Ben leaned into Lisa and nodded.

'Ben, girls, is everything all right?'

Lisa looked up.

'Mum. Yes, Tina and I and fine, Ben's not very well.'

'Poor, Ben,' said Mum, taking him into her arms and hugging him. 'Let's get you home, yes?'

Ben nodded again and hugged his mum tightly.

'Come on, girls, let's go home.'

Lisa followed her Mum out to the car. Sure, it was only half an hour, but leaving school early was a great feeling.

'We'll stop at the chemists on the way home,' said Mum, 'pick up some Calpole, oh and I need some wire wool from the handyman store.'

Lisa watched as the world sped by out of the car window.

'So, any clues to finding Mrs Jenkins's cat?'

'No, not yet, Mum, but there will be. Clue always present themselves when you least expect them,' said Tina.

Mum slowed the car to a stop outside the shops.

'Tina, stay in the car with Ben. Lisa, keep me company?'

Lisa undid her seatbelt and opened the car door, twisting in her seat to slide out.

'Be nice,' she said to Tina, who was scowling in the backseat.

'Chemist first,' said Mum.

Entering the shop, Lisa saw there were two customers in front of them, waiting to be served, so she drifted off to look at the selection of scents on the counter. When she was sure her Mum wasn't looking she picked up one of the tester bottles and sniffed it. Wrinkling her nose she put it back quickly and picked up another one.

Oh, that smells nice

She squirted a little onto each wrist and then dabbed the sides of her neck the way she had seen her Mum put on perfume. Happy and knowing Tina was going to be jealous she sprayed some onto her handkerchief, so she could smell nice too.

'It was such a shame about Old Mrs Wright getting robbed whilst she was in hospital,' said a customer to the assistant behind the counter.

'What is the world...?'

Lisa wandered around the shop, towards the selection of make-up on offer but shied away as a man picked up some flea powder from the bottom shelf whilst scratching his ankles.

Ewww, gross.

'Come on, Lisa, let's go.'

Lisa smiled and skipped over to her Mum, scratching her arm, and then her neck. Just the thought of fleas made her itchy.

'Mum, don't forget the wire wool.'

'Oh, right, thanks,' said Mum.

They walked along passed the other shops until they reached the Handy Man.

'Here we are,' said Mum.

Lisa stood with her Mum as there wasn't anything nice or fun to look at in the Handy Man shop.

'Having trouble with rats, Arthur?'

'Yeh, there's a nest of them under my shed, over the allotment.'

'Damn nuisance, but this stuff will get rid of em, no problem.'

'Let's hope so, Stan, let's hope so.'

The man took his bag from the shopkeeper and walked past Lisa, whose heart was beating really fast.

'Ok, let's go,' said Mum.

Lisa blinked. Her mind was in such a whirl she hadn't registered her Mum asking for the wire wool or paying for it or anything.

'Head in the clouds, Lisa?'

Lisa smiled. 'Just thinking.'

She leaned in close as her Mum slipped her arm around her shoulders, and together they walked back to the car.

As Lisa slid into the back seat and pulled her seat belt across her chest she whispered, "I have our first clue."

'Tell us when we get home,' Tina whispered back.

Ben who was strapped into his seat in the middle nodded his head in agreement.

'Here.' said Lisa, handing Tina her hanky, 'it's got perfume on it.'

'Ooo, thanks,' said Tina, rubbing the material behind her ears.'

Chapter Five

'Ben must be really poorly, he hasn't stopped crying since I put him to bed,' said Mum, walking into the living room. 'If he's not better by the morning, I will have to take him to the Doctors.'

Lisa looked at Tina. She knew why Ben was crying. Mum had taken him straight to bed when they got home before she could share her news and he was upset about being left out.

'Perhaps we should go up and sit with him?' she offered.

'That's kind of you, Lisa, but it's best he get some rest. The sleep will do him good.'

Lisa nodded but was only slightly mollified.

'So, our first clue,' said Tina. 'Rats. We know Twiddles was bringing rats home from his nights of hunting and we learnt today that Arthur has an allotment over run with rats.'

'We should tell Ben,' said Lisa. 'It will make him feel better.'

'Who?' said Tina. 'Oh, him. We'll tell him in the morning. We should be writing all this down,' she added.

'Why? It's not a lot. I am sure we can remember it.'

'Detectives write everything down in little notebooks, we should get some. I'll ask Dad, he's bound to have something at work he can bring home.'

'Tomorrow's Friday, we could go to the allotments after school?' suggested Lisa.

'Great idea,' said Tina. 'Oh, but we need Ben. The rats, remember?'

Lisa shuddered as she imagined the rat's beady little red eyes, their sharp pointy teeth, and their long tail. For some reason that was just as bad as their teeth and eyes.

'We definitely need Ben. If we tell him our clue, he'll stop crying. I am sure of it, and he will go to sleep and feel better in the morning.'

Lisa watched as Tina mulled it over before nodding.

'We will have to sneak up, you heard Mum, we're not to bother him.'

'Sneaking is part of being a detective,' said Lisa.

The smile that bloomed across Tina's face made Lisa chuckle.

'Come on, it's sneaking time.'

Together they left the lounge on tiptoe, pausing in the hallway as they heard their Mum moving in the kitchen, before placing the first foot on the stair. Slowly they added their weight, breathing a sigh of relief when it didn't crack or pop. In unison, they climbed the stairs, each step taken carefully.

CRAAAACCCK!

Lisa froze, her hand grabbing Tina's, her heart pounding in her chest.

Had Mum heard? Was she coming to investigate? Would they be caught?

Chapter Six

Lisa waited, expecting any moment for the kitchen door to fly open and Mum to storm out and scold them.

Finally, after what seemed an age but was really only ten seconds, Lisa breathed.

'Wow, that was close,' said Tina.

'I'd say,' said Lisa. 'Come on, next step.'

Together they placed their foot on the next step and slowly, very, very, slowly, lifted themselves upwards.

No sound.

Lisa breathed again.

Step by step, breath by breath they climbed the stairs and were finally standing on the landing.

'I never realised we had so many steps,' said Tina.

'Me neither,' said Lisa. 'I'm all sweaty.'

'Come on, let's tell Ben and get back downstairs,' said Lisa.

'Yeh, it will be just like him to get us into trouble,' said Tina.

Lisa opened Ben's bedroom door and poked her head around to check if he was asleep.

Upon seeing Lisa, Ben immediately sat up and rubbed his eyes.

Her heart gave a pang as she sat on the bed and put her arms around him.

'How are you, little man?' she asked. 'Any better?'

Ben nodded and sniffed, squeezing Lisa tight before pushing himself away.

'Tell me the clue,' he said, wiping another tear from his eye.

'Well,' said Lisa, dropping her voice low. 'In the Handyman store there was this man.'

'His name was Arthur,' said Tina, sitting on the bed and taking Ben's hand.

'And he was buying rat poison,' said Lisa.

'As he had a plague of rats under his shed,' said Tina.

'Down at his allotment,' said Lisa.

Ben followed the conversation, his head swivelling between the two as if he was watching a tennis match, his eyes wide.

'Twiddles was killing rats,' he whispered.

Lisa was impressed. Ben had made the connection immediately.

'Clever boy,' she said. 'Yes, we think Twiddles is trapped inside Arthur's shed down the allotments.'

'Probably eaten by the rats by now,' said Tina. 'But we have to check.'

'When are we going?' asked Ben.

'Well, if you're better, we're going to ask Dad to drive us there tomorrow, after school,' said Lisa.

'I will be better by then, I'm sure of it.'

'You will have to go to sleep to get better,' said Lisa.

Ben nodded and pushed himself down under his quilt and closed his eyes.

'I am sure I will be asleep any minute,' he said. 'You won't go without me will you?'

'No,' said Lisa firmly, as Tina looked up and shook her head. 'I promise.'

Tina scowled and tutted.

'Thank you,' Ben mumbled sleepily.

CREEEEEEEEK.

'It's Mum,' Lisa hissed. 'Quick hide.'

Lisa and Tina scrambled across the bed and laid flat on the ground on the other side just as the door opened.

Lisa could see all the way under the bed to the door as it opened slowly and Mum's feet stepped inside.

Convinced her Mum would hear the pounding of her heart; Lisa was amazed when her Mum moved to the side of the bed, whispered, 'Good night, my angel,' and then walked back towards the door.

They were going to get away with it. Their first time sneaking was going to be a success.

Movement caught her eye. Not much, just enough for her to clap her hand over her mouth and watch in horror.

Chapter Seven

The legs seemed to undulate as they moved one at a time, all EIGHT of them, as the huge spider advanced towards her. She was lying on the floor; her head was on the floor! And her eyes were in direct line with the SPIDER!

Mumbling, 'I'm a friend of Hagrid's,' which everyone knows is the secret password to stop spiders from eating you, cold sweat trickled down from under her arms, and she trembled as it MOVED CLOSER.

Her hand muffled her squeak but she saw her Mum's feet stop and turn. Eyes darting, and thoughts torn between Mum's wrath and the far worst danger of the spider, Lisa waited her fate. Breath held, heart pounding, Tina's hand squeezed hers every so tightly.

The feet moved first, as Mum left the room, the door closing behind her. Not a second passed before Lisa and Tina were up off the floor and onto Ben's bed, trapped, and wondering which way the spider was going to go.

'We have to move,' said Tina. 'Mum's going to find out we are not in the living room.'

Lisa, who had absolutely, positively, no intention of moving, nodded.

'What's wrong?' asked Ben, sitting up.

'Spider,' whispered Lisa.

'It won't hurt you,' said Ben.

Lisa just shook her head.

Ben sighed and threw off his duvet, and swung his legs over the side of the bed.

'Where?'

'Under the bed,' Lisa said, fear making her voice very quiet, barely a whisper.

Ben disappeared under the bed and was back in an instant, his hands cupped together.

Now many brothers would tease their sisters with a spider trapped within their hands, but not Ben. He went to the open window and threw it out.

'All gone,' he said.

'Go wash your hands,' Lisa said immediately.

Ben grinned.

Now, he might not tease his sisters with an actual spider, as they were really scared of them, but possible spider poop on his hands, well, that was another matter.

Palms outstretched, he ran at them.

Both girls screamed and jumped off the bed, out the door and thundered down the stairs, Ben's laughter following them down.

Lisa and Tina dashed to their seats and picked up their books, their breathing coming in pants, their hair plastered to their foreheads with sweat, and their cheeks flushed as they tried to act completely natural when their Mum poked her head around the door.

'All alright, girls?'

'Yes, Mum.'

The front door opened and closed and within moments, their Dad entered the living room.

'Hi Mum,' said Dad, giving Mum a kiss. 'Hi, girls, how was school?'

'Hi, Dad, it was okay.'

'Learn anything today?'

'No.'

'Nothing, you learnt nothing?'

'No.'

'How's Ben?' he asked, turning to Mum.

'Actually I think he is doing a little better,' said Mum.

Lisa gave her best innocent face as Mum looked directly at her and Tina as she spoke.

'I could have sworn I heard him laughing just now,' she added.

'Really? That's a good sign,' said Dad. 'Best keep him off tomorrow though.'

'The school suggested the same thing. It's Friday and if he is going down with something they don't want him infecting the whole school.'

'That's settled then. What's for dinner?'

The twins exchanged a look of satisfaction. They were really getting good at this Detective stuff and had clearly perfected their "innocent" face. All that time sitting in front of each other, trying to make their eyes big and their mouths open just a bit, was worth it.

Chapter Eight

The following day, the girls were excited, and the day dragged by agonizingly slowly for them. Finally, the bell sounded, and they raced out to their Mum who was waiting with the other Mums to collect them.

Standing with her was Ben, looking happy and excited as he waved the moment he saw them.

Lisa waved back and soon they were all heading home.

'How was school?'

'Okay.'

'Learn anything?'

'Nope.'

'Dad's already home,' said Ben excitedly.

'Really, great,' said Tina. 'We can go as soon as we get home.'

'I think he's as excited as you three,' said Mum laughing. 'He even came home early from work.'

'Do we need to take anything with us?' Lisa asked quietly to Tina.

'Like what?'

'I don't know, that's why I'm asking.'

'Cat treats,' said Ben. 'In case we have to coax Twiddles out of the shed.'

'Great idea,' said Lisa, ruffling Ben's hair. 'Clever boy.'

'Mum we need some cat treats,' said Tina.

'What? Why?'

'To coax out Twiddles,' said Ben.

'Ummmmm, I am sure Mrs Jenkins will have some. We can ask her.'

Lisa and Tina nodded.

Jumping out of the car, the twins raced for the house.

'DAD! DAD! We're home. Can we go now?'

'Wait for me!' yelled Ben, struggling in his seat, as he was securely strapped in.

'Calm down, no one is going anywhere without you,' said Mum.

Lisa waited at the door so Ben could see her and smiled as he ran from the car, past her, into the house.

'Good girl,' said Mum as she walked passed Lisa, patting her on the arm.

Beaming, Lisa rushed upstairs to change out of her school uniform.

*

'What's keeping him?' asked Lisa.

'I told you we shouldn't have included him,' said Tina.

'You did no such thing.'

'Well I thought it.'

'Calm down you two,' said Dad. 'He'll be down in just a moment.'

They all turned their heads at the sound of footsteps coming down the stairs.

The door opened and Lisa looked on agog.

'What do you think?' asked Ben, standing there dressed in a light brown mackintosh, with a belt tied around his waist, sun glasses over his eyes and a hat upon his head. He looked like a secret agent.

'You looked fabulous, Ben,' said Dad. 'Good job, Mum.'

'Nice work with the hat,' said Mum. 'It's a perfect fit.'

A wave of jealousy washed through Lisa and she knew Tina was feeling the same. You didn't need to be her twin either, it was written all over her face.

'That's not fair,' said Tina. 'Why does he get a secret agent outfit?'

'He looks great, Mum, really good job,' said Lisa, spotting the firm line of Mum's lips. She nudged Tina with her elbow.

'Ow! What's that for?' said Tina, rubbing her arm.

'Say something nice,' she hissed back, trying to smile at the same time.

'You look really great, Ben,' said Tina. Turning to Lisa she asked, 'Have we got anything we can wear as good as that?'

'Mum's got outfits for you too,' said Ben, his feet dancing on the spot. 'We've been shopping all day, and Dad got the hats, aren't they cool?'

Lisa and Tina raced each other as the rushed to hug Mum and then Dad and then Mum again, squealing with delight.

'Where are they? Are they upstairs? I bet they're upstairs.'

Lisa watched her Mum closely; Tina's outburst might have spoiled everything.

'They're in my room. You can go and put them on, then Dad will take you to the allotments.'

'YEHHHHH!' yelled Tina, dashing out of the room.

'Thanks, Mum,' said Lisa again, before chasing after Tina, Ben right behind her.

'Ben, why don't you wait down here,' suggested Dad, moving swiftly to catch him before he bolted up the stairs.

Ben looked up the stairs then at his Dad.

'We can go and ask Mrs Jenkins if she has any cat treats.'

Ben's face lit up and he pulled out his wallet.

'Detective Sergeant Ben O'Brien.'

Chapter Nine

'Man, those treats stink,' said Tina.

'Fish,' said Lisa. 'Makes sense, as they're for cats, I mean.'

'Dare you to eat one,' said Tina to Ben.

Ben's eyes lit up as his hand dived into the box.

'No!' said Dad, from the front seat. 'No eating the cat treats. They will make you sick. Tina, stop daring your brother into doing stuff like that.'

Tina grinned.

'Tina.'

'Yeeeeeees, Dad,' Tina said, rolling her eyes at Lisa.

'There are the allotments,' said Ben, pointing out the window.

A surge of excitement tingled through Lisa, as she saw the rows of small gardens lined up, filled with vegetables and vines hanging off canes, each one with its own shed.

'Which one is Arthur's?' asked Tina.

'We will have to search all of them I guess,' said Lisa.

Dad parked the car and the girls and Ben piled out of the back, pulling on their trench coats and hats, eager to get going.

'Now, you can't just go running around the allotment,' said Dad. 'Make sure you ask permission before you search anyone's shed, is that clear?'

'Yes, Dad,' said Lisa, Tina, and Ben solemnly.

'Do you all have your identification cards and badges? Let me see 'em'

Lisa dug hers out of the pocket in her trench coat and flipped it open, smiling in delight as the badge caught the light and shone brightly.

'Good good, off you go, be polite, and remember, Twiddles might be scared, so be careful not to get scratched.'

Lisa nodded and followed Tina who had darted off the moment Dad had said, 'Off you go.'

Tina had raced off, leaving her and Ben behind, so Lisa decided to talk to the nearest gardener.

'Excuse me, Sir,' said Lisa, flashing her badge. 'I'm with the O'Brien Detective Agency, and we are searching for a lost cat. Could you tell me which allotment belongs to Arthur?'

The man straightened his back and scratched his head. 'Arthur you say? Not in any trouble is he?'

'No, Sir. We understand he has a rat problem.'

'Rat problem is it. That'll be Art then, his garden's the last one on the end there.'

'Thank you, Sir.'

Lisa and Ben moved towards the last allotment at the end, waving Tina over as she came out of a shed, in one of the other allotments.

'Found it,' said Lisa, as Tina came running over.

'Cool, which one?'

'That one,' said Lisa, pointing.

They made it to Arthur's shed, which stood in a small patch of ground.

'We'll wait here,' said Lisa, giving Ben a gentle shove in the back. 'Go on then, take a look,' she added.

'Are you coming with me?' said Ben.

Both girls shook their heads.

'There are rats in there,' said Tina.

Lisa waited anxiously as she watched Ben walk around the shed, testing the door.

'The door is locked,' he called back. 'But there's a loose board here.'

'Be careful,' Lisa called out.

She watched as Ben lifted the board up and stuck his head inside, then wriggled his body through the narrow opening.

The sound of a cat's meow was clearly heard.

'We did it,' said Tina grabbing Lisa's arm. 'We solved the case.'

Lisa nodded, watching the shed intently, willing Ben to emerge unscathed and quickly. The idea of Arthur coming along just as success was in their grasp teased her thoughts.

'Grab Twiddles,' Ben called out, his head suddenly appearing from the small opening, one hand holding the cat.

'You go,' said Tina, giving Lisa a push.

'Why me?' said Lisa.

'You're older,' said Tina.

'We're twins,' said Lisa.

'Older is older,' said Tina, 'and you were born first, now go.'

Lisa frowned, but the cat's twisting and turning, as it squirmed to get out of Ben's hands, made up her mind and she dashed forward.

The cat managed to get free and crouched low, hissing at Lisa as she approached.

The production of the cat treats changed Twiddles temperament from angry to cordial instantly and she padded over and nibbled the treats from Lisa's palm.

Lisa picked her up and stroked her fur, further calming her until she purred.

Ben's head appeared looking left and right, relief clear on his face when he saw Lisa had Twiddles safe and sound.

Pulling himself out of the shed, he stood dusting himself off, settled his hat squarely on his head, and walked over.

'The name's O'Brien, Ben O'Brien.'

Lisa laughed and hugged him with her free arm.

'Well done. Good job.'

Ben seemed to swell in front of her, as he stood up straighter and puffed out his chest, and positively beamed.

Tina came over and took the cat from Lisa.

'Didn't Ben do well?' said Lisa.

'He did ok,' said Tina, turning her back and walking back through the allotments towards their Dad and the car.

Lisa turned to Ben as he deflated a little, his eyes watery as he watched her go.

'I think you did a great job,' she said putting her arm back around his shoulders. 'Come on; let's get Twiddles back to Mrs Jenkins. I bet she is going to be so happy.'

Ben smiled.

'Thanks, Lisa.'

Together they walked back to the car, Tina up in front, cat in one hand, scratching an itch on her leg with the other.

Chapter Ten

Mrs Jenkins was delighted. She hugged each of them *twice*, and insisted they take the five-pound note she had offered as a reward, despite their Dad refusing at first.

Lisa was in two minds about that. On one hand, it did feel a little mean to take money from an old lady. Mrs Jenkins's happiness was such a pleasure to see, she felt fully rewarded. On the other hand, if they were to be proper detectives then they should accept the rewards offered. Happy to leave it up to her Dad to make the final decision she was still a little open mouthed when Tina plucked the five pound note from her Dad's hand and tucked it into the pocket of her trench coat.

Trooping back home, Lisa felt tired. Detective work was hard and hungry work.

'So, kids, what are you planning to do with your money?' asked Dad.

'Spend it,' said Tina immediately. 'Lisa and I are going to buy some make-up. Mum said we could.'

'And how are you dividing up the money?' said Dad.

'Two pound fifty each,' said Tina.

'What about Ben?'

'What about him?'

'Dad's right. Ben deserves some,' said Lisa.

'And he does work for you, remember,' said Dad. 'You have to pay your employees first.'

Tina frowned as she considered this.

'We should divide it equally,' said Lisa.

'That's ok. You can keep it all. I'm just glad you let me join in,' said Ben.

'There, he doesn't want any,' said Tina. 'Sorted.'

'Another way is to invest the money in the business,' said Dad. 'Didn't you mention you all need notebooks?'

'That's right,' said Lisa. 'We should use the money for that. That way it's fair and we all benefit.'

'Notebooks?' said Tina, looking at the money in her hand. 'I don't want to buy notebooks. I want to buy lipstick.'

'Well, whatever you decide to use the money for; the business; those hats and coats weren't free you know, or treat yourselves to something nice, Ben has to have his share,' said Dad firmly.

'We have to pay for the hats and coats?' asked Tina.

Lisa looked at her Mum. She had worked out ages ago to watch her Mum when having fun with Dad. Whilst she was smiling, as she was now, it was ok. When the smile disappeared, it was time to stop teasing him. You wouldn't believe how quickly fun and laughter could turn to being sent to bed and no Friday night treat.

Usually because Tina would say something rude or get silly about Dad's teasing.

'Yes, but it doesn't have to be money,' said Dad. 'There are other ways to pay.'

Lisa smelt a rat, not literally of course, but figuratively. Dad was up to something, she was sure of it.

'Will do that then,' said Tina.

'Hang on,' said Lisa. 'What do you have in mind?'

'A photo,' said Dad, 'of the three of you, together, hats, and coats, with you flashing your badges.'

Chapter Eleven

Lisa shook her head sadly and looked at Tina, who was clearly considering it.

'Tina!' she said indignantly.

Having their photo taken together was something they both agreed on. NEVER AGAIN! Too many photos of them growing up already existed, far too many for her liking and nearly all, but the most recent ones, had them dressed exactly the same. She shuddered.

'Just one photo,' said Tina.

'Ten,' countered Dad.

'No way,' said Lisa.

'If it's only one, you will pull faces and spoil it. I'll need to take ten to get one good one.'

Tina and Lisa huddled together. Ben stuck his head under Lisa's arm.

'What do you think?' asked Tina.

'It's a trap,' said Lisa. 'If we weaken, Dad and Mum will be taking photos all the time.'

'It would be good to have photos of us being detectives,' said Ben, 'for our files.'

'Shut up, this doesn't concern you,' said Tina.

'Yes it does,' Ben snapped back.

'He has a point,' said Lisa, her mind turning over the idea of a photo record of their sleuthing. It would have been nice to have had a photo of Ben coming out of the shed with the cat; he looked so cute with his hat all wonky. 'How about...?'

The three of them huddled close and discussed the matter seriously. It took a good five minutes before they nodded and moved apart.

'Ok, we will allow you to take a photo and we will smile. But, we get a copy for our records and if we let you take photos of us solving our cases, we get a copy of those too.'

'Done,' said Dad. 'I will be your official photographer.'

Lisa stuck out her hand and Dad shook it.

Ben stuck his hand out too, and laughing, Dad shook his hand as well.

Tina spat on her hand and held it out.

'Tina! That's not very lady like,' said Mum.

'It's how it's done,' said Tina. 'I've seen it on TV.'

Dad spat on his hand grasped Tina's firmly and shook it.

Lisa smiled. Tina didn't look so pleased with herself now she had to shake Dad's hand with his spit all over it and she wiped her hand on Ben's shoulder immediately afterwards.

'Stand together,' said Dad. 'Flash your badges.'

Twenty-five photos later, Lisa and Tina finally agreed they had one they would accept; even Dad was complaining that it was taking forever in the end.

'So,' Dad said, 'what's our next case?'

Lisa looked at Dad. 'Our?'

'Sure, I'm your driver and official photographer so I should be a detective too. Junior detective, obviously.'

Lisa looked at Mum who was laughing quietly.

'You're enjoying this as much as the kids,' Mum said.

'I am,' said Dad, reaching behind the armchair, pulling out a hat and placing it on his head. 'I bought this when I was getting the hats for the kids. I got you one too,' he added, pulling out a second hat and spinning it through the air.

Mum caught it deftly and placed it on her head.

'How do I look?' she asked, twisting this way and that, as she modelled it.

'Really great, Mum,' said Lisa, and meant it. The hat really suited her.

'Awww thanks.'

'So, next case?'

'Nothing yet, but there's sure to be one soon,' said Lisa.

How right she was.

Chapter Twelve

'Tina, why do you keep scratching your legs?' asked Mum.

'They itch. Something's bit me.'

'Let me see.'

Lisa, who was sitting next to Tina on the sofa, noticed loads of little red marks on Tina's legs as she showed her Mum.

'Those are flea bites.'

'Fleas!' squealed Lisa, throwing herself over the arm of the sofa.

Ben, who had been sitting the other side of Tina, dived onto the floor, rolling several times theatrically.

Tina jumped up slapping her legs.

'Get them off, get them off,' she screamed.

'Calm down,' said Mum. 'I'm not saying you have fleas, just flea bites. Where have you been?'

'Nowhere the others haven't,' said Tina.

Mum looked at Lisa.

'I haven't got any bites,' said Lisa.

Lisa pushed her socks down and showed her bare legs, free of any bites.

'Me, neither,' said Ben, pulling his trouser leg up.

'Lisa, go get me the Calamine lotion. Tina, you mustn't scratch or they will get infected.'

'Cheer up,' said Lisa. 'At least tomorrow is Saturday and you won't have to go to school with your legs covered in this stuff.'

Tina nodded, looking miserable.

'So where have you been, where there are fleas, I mean?' said Mum.

'Only the allotment,' said Tina.

'Well, Ben and I are ok, so it couldn't have been Arthur's shed.'

'It must have been that one with all the bikes,' said Tina.

'Bikes?' said Ben.

Tina nodded.

'Well never mind that now,' said Mum. 'This will stop the itching and they will soon clear up.'

'Daddy's home!' cried Ben, leaping up and running to the door.

'Hi, sport.'

Lisa threw her arms around Dad as he entered the lounge carrying Ben.

'Hi, Dad.'

'Hi, princess. No hugs from you, sweetness?'

'I've got fleas,' said Tina sadly.

'Oh?' said Dad, looking at Mum.

'She hasn't *got* fleas,' said Mum. 'Just flea bites.'

'Oh,' said Dad. 'Come here then,' he said putting Ben down and sweeping Tina up in his arms.

Lisa smiled as Tina squealed and shrieked as Dad tipped her head down towards the floor.

'Busy day?' asked Mum.

Lisa caught the glance Dad threw Mum and her pulse raced.

'Come on,' she said, 'let's go play.'

'Me too?' asked Ben.

'You too,' said Lisa, grabbing Ben and tickling him.

He giggled and squirmed before escaping and racing off upstairs.

Tina straightened her clothes as she cast a curious look towards Lisa, one she met with a stare and slight nod.

Tina nodded. 'Let's play hide and seek.'

'Be nice to your brother,' said Dad.

Lisa avoided looking at her Dad as she said, 'We will.'

The last time they had played hide and seek with Ben, well every time they had played actually, they had sent him off to hide, then played with their toys.

A small smile tugged at Lisa's lips.

Ben would hide for ages before he would realise. Every time! Seriously dim that boy.

Chapter Thirteen

'You two hide and I will seek,' said Ben, the moment Lisa and Tina entered their room.

Smart boy, Lisa thought.

'We're not really playing,' said Lisa, adding quickly when she saw Ben's face fall. 'Not yet, anyway. Dad's worried about something in work. That could mean a case for us to solve.'

'Ohhhhh, clever,' said Tina.

Ben's eyes sparkled.

'What do we do?' he asked.

'Sneak down the stairs and listen,' said Lisa in a whisper.

'We'll get into trouble,' said Ben.

'Baby,' said Tina.

'I'm not a baby,' said Ben.

Lisa frowned at Tina.

'We'll only get into trouble if we're caught,' she said. 'So let's not get caught. Besides, we're detectives, we're supposed to detect.'

Watching Ben think it over was so adorable, Lisa wanted to hug him, as it was; she forced herself to sit and watch as he thought about it, chewing his bottom lip, a sure sign of deep concentration.

Tina on the other hand was up and ready to go. Consequences or not, she didn't care, it was exciting.

Ben looked up at Lisa and nodded. 'I'm in.'

Lisa nodded back, feeling a surge of frustration as Tina tutted.

'Remember how we all crawled down the stairs the other week, on our tummies? Let's do that.'

'Good plan,' said Tina, 'they will never spot us.'

Lisa opened the bedroom door and looked out.

'All clear,' she whispered.

'We need to work out hand signals,' said Tina.

'What, now?' asked Lisa.

'No, not now, idiot, later.'

Lisa bridled at 'idiot' but she swallowed it down.

'And a code, so we can send each other secret messages,' said Ben.

'Actually, that's a great idea,' said Tina. 'Good thinking.'

Lisa smiled as she watched Ben's face light up as Tina ruffled his hair.

'What are you smiling at?' asked Tina.

'Nothing,' said Lisa. 'Come on.'

Lisa slipped out the door and along the landing towards the stairs, the muffled sounds of her parents talking filtering up from below.

'I'll go first,' said Tina, moving past Lisa and lowering herself to the ground.

Head first; she crawled down the stairs, using her arms to take her weight. Lisa went next, and she felt Ben bump into her legs and knew he was right behind her.

'These burglaries have us stumped,' said Dad. 'We are sure of our suspects but cannot prove it. If only we could connect one of them to the thefts, we could question him about how they are communicating and coordinating their raids.'

'Sounds dangerous,' said Mum.

'No, not really. These men are rough but not violent. I'd really like to catch them before the holidays.'

'Have you told the kids were we're going?'

'No not yet. They will be so excited when we tell them.'

Tina looked back at Lisa and pointed.

Lisa nodded and looked back at Ben.

'Back up.'

Ben nodded and pushed himself back up the stairs. He had only gone down two steps, so it didn't take him long.

Lisa pushed herself backwards and was soon waiting at the top for Tina.

'Back to HQ,' said Tina, going to the bedroom.

Ben and Lisa followed and sat on Lisa's bed whilst Tina paced the room.

'Where do you think we're going?' she said.

'Going?' asked Lisa.

'On holiday. You heard Dad; it's going to be somewhere exciting.'

'Disneyland,' said Ben excitedly.

Tina's eyes flashed with excitement before she flicked her hair.

'That's a silly idea,' she said. 'We cannot afford that. I heard Mummy saying the other day how expensive everything was getting. Besides, Lisa and I are too old for Disneyland.'

Lisa placed her hand on Ben's shoulder, who had puffed up, ready for an outburst that would only lead to yelling, which in turn would get them all into trouble.

'Wherever it is, we need to help Daddy solve his case. He'll be so much more fun if he's not distracted by work.'

Tina opened her mouth to say something, then closed it, thought for a second, then said, 'True.'

'So what do we know?' Lisa said, standing up and going over to the chalkboard.

'Burglaries,' said Tina. 'Dad mentioned there have been a lot of burglaries.'

'Secret communication,' said Ben.

'What?' said Tina. 'This is not a game, these are real criminals.'

'No, wait, Ben is right. Dad mentioned they wanted to catch one of the thieves so he could tell them how they were communicating and coordinating with each other,' said Lisa.

'See,' said Ben.

'I must have missed that,' said Tina, chewing her finger. 'Sorry, Ben. How do we find out more about the burglaries? Dad's not going to tell us.'

They all thought for a bit.

'The newspapers,' said Lisa. 'The local one for sure will have something on them, and Mum has a pile of them for recycling.'

'It's going to look a bit odd if we start reading the newspaper,' said Tina, 'and you know Mum will forbid us to investigate. She already thinks it's dangerous.'

'Do you think it's dangerous?' asked Ben.

Lisa shook her head.

'Not for us, no. We're not going to arrest them or anything. Just find the clues to help Daddy.'

Ben chewed his bottom lip.

'What's on your mind, Ben?' asked Lisa.

'Paper mache,' said Ben.

Lisa frowned but Tina clapped her hands.

'That's brilliant. Oh, why didn't I think of that? If we tell Mum we want to make some paper mache masks, she will give us all the newspapers. We can read them and have fun making masks at the same time.'

Chapter Thirteen

Lisa loved the gloopy mess between her fingers as she and Ben made their masks, whilst Tina scanned the papers for any news of the burglaries.

They had quite a pile of clippings already, having agreed that they would read them through thoroughly together after they had made their masks. These were key to keeping up their rouse and far too much fun in the making to pass up the opportunity.

'Okay, that's the lot,' said Tina, pushing the clippings to one side, as she tore up the last of the paper for their masks.

'Well, I've finished,' said Lisa. 'Why don't I start reading through them, whilst you get cracking with your mask.'

Lisa could see the indecision on Tina's face. Tina loved paper mache, but she didn't want to miss out on finding any clues either.

'I've finished too,' said Ben. 'I can read some.'

'How about we read them aloud?' said Lisa. 'That way Ben can practice his reading and Tina can listen as she works.'

Tina's smile was all toothy it was so broad.

'Ooooo, lovely,' said Tina, as she placed her hands into the glue.

Ben settled himself in front of Lisa and picked up the first clipping.

'The Jewellers in the High Road is the fifth shop to be burgled this month,' Ben said, as he traced the words with his fingers.

'The raids are carefully..., what's that word?'

'Orc... es...trated,' said Lisa, running her finger under the word so Ben could see how to break it down.

'The raids are carefully orch es trated,' Ben repeated, 'with the robbers escaping with thousands of pounds of watches and rings. A reward of one thousand pound for any information leading to their capture is on offer.

Together with the other rewards, the total now stands at four thousand five hundred pounds.'

'So much?' said Lisa, looking at Tina, 'We could give it to Mummy to help out with food and stuff.'

'Read another,' said Tina, plastering her balloon with strips of gluey paper.

'Here's one that looks interesting,' said Lisa, handing it to Ben.

'The Evans family were in for a shock when they opened their door, after coming home from their holidays, as their house had been burgled.'

'Well, that *is* interesting,' said Tina. 'Have our shop thieves moved on to homes, or are they unconnected do you think?'

'May I?' asked Lisa, taking the clipping from Ben. 'It goes on to say the police have no clues to work on presently, as there were no finger prints at the scene and no witnesses. As yet, none of the stolen items have been seen.'

'What does that mean?' asked Ben. 'If they were stolen, why would they be seen?'

'Good question,' said Tina. 'The thieves would most likely sell anything they have stolen, so what the reporter means is, none of the stolen items have shown up in pawn shops or those money shops yet.'

Ben looked up at Lisa. 'What's a pawn shop?'

'It's a place where you can get money for your valuables,' said Lisa.

'But they won't sell them for three months or something,' said Tina. 'In case you want them back.'

'Dad says they have suspects but cannot tell how they are communicating with each other,' said Lisa. 'If we can crack that, he will be able to arrest them.'

'But we don't know who those suspects are,' said Tina.

Lisa pulled at her bottom lip.

'Should I read some more?' asked Ben.

'Yes, keep reading, Ben,' said Tina.

'Listen to this,' said Ben. 'One of the most....' Ben looked up at Lisa.

'Audacious,' said Lisa.

'Robberies,' Ben continued, 'was the theft of the bicycles from the local bike shop as it was carried out in broad daylight. I heard about that. The receptionists were talking about it. That's it, that's how we help Daddy.'

'I don't get it. How does that help us?' said Tina.

'Fleas,' said Ben. 'Or flea bites really. You said you saw a shed full of bikes down the allotment.'

'That's true,' said Tina. 'Well done. This has to help Dad. He can arrest the owner and interrogate him. I am sure he can get him to talk.'

'Let's go and tell him,' said Lisa, leaping up.

'Wait for me,' said Tina, wiping her hands frantically as Lisa and Ben raced out of the room.

Chapter Fourteen

'Dad, Dad,' yelled Lisa, thundering down the stairs.

'Wait for me,' screeched Tina, taking the stairs two at a time.

Ben was jumping up and down, tugging at Dad's jumper.

'Calm down everyone,' ordered Dad. 'Count to ten.'

Tina opened her mouth to speak.

'Arh, not a word, young lady. Count.'

Tina closed her mouth and silent counted ten. Really fast.

'Now, Lisa, why don't you tell me what's got you so excited?'

'We solved your case,' said Lisa excitedly. 'Well, we have a lead. That's what it's called, right?'

'Let me hear it and I will tell you,' said Dad.

'The stolen bikes,' Tina blurted out. 'We know where they are.'

'Really,' said Dad, standing and pacing the room. 'Go on, leave nothing out.'

'When we rescued Twiddles,' said Lisa.

'The cat,' said Ben.

'Tina went to another allotment and there was a shed full of bicycles in it.'

'And fleas,' added Ben.

'So if you know who owns that allotment,' said Tina.

'We can arrest him for having the bicycles,' said Dad. 'Well done, girls, well done, Ben. This is indeed a lead.'

Dad walked out of the room and the girls hugged each other as they heard him on the phone.

They all crowded round Dad when he came back into the room.

'Let me in at least,' Dad said, laughing. 'Everyone to the table and I will tell you what's happening.'

Lisa let go her arms from around his waist as did Tina, and Ben let go of his leg, each rushing to the table to claim a seat.

'Wait for me,' cried Mum from the kitchen, making a brief appearance, as she wiped her hands on a dishtowel, to enforce her words.

Dad smiled and took his seat at the head of the table and remained silent, shaking his head at the barrage of questions Lisa and the others threw at him.

'At least tell us...............'

'Can you just nod or shake your head...?'

'Wink or smile,' said Ben. 'He smiled, he smiled. He knows who the flea man is.'

'Ok, I'm ready,' said Mum, walking through from the kitchen baring two cups of tea. One, she placed in front of Dad, the other, she held as she sat down, and sighed pleasurably as she took a sip.

'Well, to answer your questions in order,' said Dad. 'Yes, we are sending someone over to check if the bicycles are still on the allotment. Yes, if this leads to the arrest of the whole gang, you will be entitled to the reward money and no, we do not know *yet* who the flea man is.'

'Are we likely to find out anymore tonight?' asked Mum.

Dad shook his head.

'I might get a call later about the allotment but that's about it for today. Tomorrow we can really get going, track down the allotment owner, and quiz him about his friends. With any luck we can have the whole case wrapped up before the holidays.'

Lisa's heart dropped, as she knew what was coming next.

'Time for bed then,' Mum announced, standing up.

'But Mum,' Lisa whined, 'can't we stay up a little longer, in case they phone back with news. I am sure we won't get a wink of sleep until we know.'

'No, it's a school day tomorrow and you will be sleepy heads in the morning if you stay up late.'

'We won't. We promise,' said Tina. 'Pleaaaaaaase.'

Lisa held her breath as her Mum looked at her Dad.

'If they are ready for bed,' said Dad, 'and...'

Lisa, Tina, and Ben cheered, throwing their arms around Mum and Dad, colliding with each other as they raced from one to the other before tearing off up the stairs to change for bed.

'AND CLEAN YOUR TEETH,' Mum yelled up the stairs.

Chapter Fifteen

The next day seemed to drag by. True to their word, they were not sleepy at all, as they were far too excited to get home and find out if their Dad had arrested the flea man. All three breaks during their school day, Lisa and Tina went outside to find Ben to talk about the case.

Home time finally came, and they rushed out of the building as if it were on fire.

'Have you heard anything?' yelled Tina, the moment she saw Mum.

'Is Daddy home yet?' Lisa called out, trying to run, pull her bag onto her shoulder, and carry her artwork, all at the same time.

'Hi, Mum,' said Ben, waving.

'Well, at least one of you remembered to say Hi,' said Mum, sweeping Ben up into her arms and giving him a big kiss on the cheek with additional sound effects too boot.

'MMMMMMMMMMMMWAH!'

Lisa and Tina looked at each other smugly.

'That's because you would have done that to us!' said Tina, laughing as Ben pulled down his T-shirt and smoothed his hair, his cheeks bright red.

'Muuuummm, not in front of everybody,' said Ben.

'Hi, Mum,' said Lisa. 'How was your day?'

That sounded very grown up to Lisa, and she smiled, very pleased with herself.

'Great, Lisa. How about yours, learn anything interesting today?'

'Nope,' said Lisa, climbing into the car.

'What? Nothing? Ever? Every day I ask and every day you say nope,' said Mum, rolling her eyes.

'We told you. Going to school is a waste of time. We should be working with Dad, solving cases,' said Tina.

'How about you, Ben, did you learn anything today?'

Ben looked at Tina and Lisa before answering.

'Nope,' he said, and burst out laughing.

Mum laughed too.

'Well, I learnt something, but I guess if you three are not learning anything today, then I'm not sharing.'

'Is it about the case?' said Tina immediately.

'Come on, Mum, what is it?' said Lisa.

'I'll trade you,' said Mum. 'You tell me something you learned today and I will tell you what I have.'

Tina and Lisa exchanged glances, both narrowing their eyes as they tried to think of a way to get the information without having to give any.

'I learnt my eight times table,' said Ben.

'Cool, let's hear it then,' said Mum.

'One times eight is eight; two times eight is sixteen............'

Ben recited the eight times table up to twelve times eight before stopping.

'Yeh!' cheered Mum. 'That was great, Ben. Lisa, what have you got for me?'

'Well, Mrs Greenway was talking about the Great Fire of London,' said Lisa.

'Which was when?' said Mum.

'Sixteen sixty six,' said Tina.

'I'm telling it,' said Lisa. 'It started in Pudding Lane, in a bakery.'

'How did they put it out?'

'They pulled down people's houses,' said Tina.

'To create fire breaks,' added Lisa. 'But the Mayor of London left it too late and the fire swept across London.'

'It raged all day Monday and continued into Tuesday,' said Tina. 'Fighting broke out between the English, French, and Dutch residents.'

'St Paul's was destroyed, and the fire was finally stopped by the Tower of London soldiers using gunpowder to blow up houses, warehouses, and stuff so the fire had nothing to burn.'

'Wow,' said Mum, 'that was some fire.'

'It was huge,' said Tina.

'Though not many people were reported to have died,' said Lisa. 'Only six died officially.'

'I'm surprised it was so few, a fire of that size, spreading across most of London,' said Mum.

'Mrs Greenway said the poor and homeless deaths weren't recorded and many might have burnt to ash, the flames were so hot,' said Tina.

'My goodness, they must have been very hot,' said Mum. 'Well, my news is...'

The girls lent forward as far as their seat belts allowed.

'Your Dad phoned to say...'

'Come on, Muuuuuuum,' said Tina. 'Out with it.'

'They found the shed with the bikes, so they've been recovered and taken away to a safe place, thanks to you three.'

'Yes!' cried Tina, offering up her hand to high five, first to Lisa and then to Ben.

'But they don't know who put them there as the man who owns the allotment knew nothing about them.'

'He's lying,' said Tina. 'Arrest him and make him talk.'

'Yes,' said Lisa. 'Shine a bright light in his face until he confesses.'

Mum laughed.

'I don't think your Dad would approve of that, Lisa, besides, the owner is ninety seven, a little old to be stealing bikes, and he has an alibi.'

'What's that mean?' asked Ben.

'Alibi?' said Mum. 'It's proof you were elsewhere when the crime was committed.'

'So where was he then?' asked Tina. 'Can he prove it?'

'He was in a nursing home,' said Mum. 'He had had a fall and needed care.'

'Oh,' said Tina. 'Is he all right now?'

'Yes, he's fine.'

'That's good,' said Lisa. 'So who put the bikes in his shed?'

Tina and Lisa lapsed into silence as they thought.

'I know my seven times table too,' said Ben. 'One times seven is seven. Two...'

Chapter Sixteen

'DAD'S HOME.'

Lisa and Tina jumped up, tore out of their room, and raced down the stairs, Ben just behind them.

'Dad!' squealed Lisa, launching herself at Dad as he sat on the sofa.

'OOOOOAF!' complained Dad. 'You're getting to big for that.'

Just as he moved Lisa to one side, Tina came barrelling in, and threw herself at Dad, leaping into the air to land onto his lap.

'OOOOOOOUFF!'

'Tina, my gawd!' said Dad.

Tina slide off to Dad's right as Lisa was already on the left and slide her arms around his waist.

'Got anymore news?' she asked.

'Hiya, kiddo,' said Dad, as Ben climbed onto his lap.

'Hiya, Dad,' said Ben.

'So you want some news?'

'Yes!' pleaded Tina. 'There must be more to tell, you've been at work for ages!'

'Well, there is a little, not much mind, but a little.'

'Tell us. Tell us.'

'Well, we recovered the bikes and the Bike shop owner is so please he has agreed to give you the reward even though the thieves have not been caught yet.'

'YEH!' said Tina, Lisa, and Ben, fists pumping the air as they raised their arms in celebration.

'How much?' said Tina.

'One hundred pounds,' said Dad.

'Ohhhhhh, so much. We can buy lots of make-up now,' said Tina.

'I was thinking you could open a bank account with the reward money,' said Dad.

'A bank account, like you and Mummy have?' asked Ben.

'Yes, exactly like that.'

'I like that idea,' said Lisa.

'Me too,' said Ben.

'But we can spend the money?' asked Tina. 'It is ours.'

Dad nodded.

'It is, but Mummy and I cannot let you spend one hundred pounds on make-up. Besides, a third of that money belongs to Ben.'

'That's ok, Lisa and Tina can have it,' said Ben.

'Don't you want to be able to buy things?' asked Dad.

Ben shook his head.

'Mummy buys my things for me.'

Dad laughed.

'That's true, but wouldn't you like to buy your own things? Take the fire truck you want for your birthday.'

'The big red one?' said Ben, bouncing on Dad's lap, 'with the working hoses and everything?'

'Yes, that one. Wouldn't you like to buy that for yourself?'

'I want it for my birthday,' said Ben.

'How about buying it now, with your own money?' said Dad.

'But what about my birthday? I wouldn't have any presents.'

'You would, you would have something else.'

'But I want the fire truck,' said Ben, sticking out his bottom lip, his bright blue eyes filling with tears. 'Can't I have that?'

'Of course you can,' said Mum. 'Dad, stop confusing the boy.'

'I was trying to explain...' said Dad.

'I know, but he is too young.'

'I am not,' said Ben immediately. 'I'm nearly six.'

'Yes, sweetie, I know.'

'And I still get my fire truck? For my birthday?'

'Yes, dear.'

Ben smiled.

'Is there anything else?' asked Lisa. 'Have you found the flea man?'

Dad shook his head.

'Not yet, no.'

'Well the O'Brien Detective Agency is on the case,' declared Tina. 'We will find him.'

'You will do no such things,' said Mum. 'You leave that to the police. How about the park? You like the park; I'll take you there tomorrow.'

'Yeh!' said Ben.

Tina and Lisa looked at each other.

I love the park, thought Lisa.

But I want to work on the case, thought Tina.

We can work on the case when we get home, thought Lisa.

Tina nodded.

Lisa nodded.

'The park it is,' said Tina.

Chapter Seventeen

'Faster, faster,' squealed Ben, as he spun round and round.

'You'll be sick,' warned Mum.

'No we won't,' shrieked Lisa, as she held on tightly. She loved the rush of air on her face and how it took her breath away.

'Weeeeeeeeeeeeee,' screamed Tina, as she threw her head back.

Finally, Mum was exhausted.

'I need to sit down,' said Mum.

Lisa, Tina, and Ben laughed hysterically as they tried to walk in a straight line, stumbling and falling over, only to stagger to their feet, and try again.

Tired out, Lisa lay on the grass, panting. She turned her head away from the bright blue cloudless sky and looked out over the park and her heart quickened.

'Tina, Tina,' she hissed.

'What,' said Tina lazily, one arm over her eyes to shade it from the hot beating sun.

'The flea man.'

Tina and Ben both sat up, looking about wildly.

'That's not very covert,' said Lisa, sitting up.

Tina didn't answer as she watched the only other person nearby take a seat on the park bench and pull his newspaper from under his arm.

'That's him? Over by the bench?'

Lisa nodded.

'He's the man in the Chemists that bought the flea powder. He has to be part of the criminal gang.'

'We need to get closer,' said Tina. 'See if there are any identifying marks we can tell Dad about.'

'Let's go and play on the swings,' said Ben.

'Not now, Ben, we're on a case,' said Lisa.

'No, he's right,' said Tina. 'The swings are in front of the man. They will allow us to get close enough without giving ourselves away. Good thinking, Ben.'

Lisa looked at Tina in amazement.

'What?' asked Tina quizzically.

Lisa smiled.

'Nothing. Well done, Ben.'

They pushed themselves up off the grass and raced over to the swings.

'I'll push you, Ben,' said Lisa loudly.

'Don't overdo it,' said Tina quietly.

Lisa nodded; even she was startled at how loud that had come out.

'Higher, higher,' Ben cried, as he kicked his legs, urging the swing to soar into the sky.

Lisa pushed harder, all the time looking across the park to the bench and their suspect.

'Hold on tight, Ben,' said Tina, as she swung back and forth, encouraging her own swing to greater heights.

'Come on, kids, time we got going,' yelled Mum.

Tina leapt off mid swing and flew through the air towards the man.

'TINA!' yelled Mum, running over.

Landing perfectly, Tina, with a broad smile, turned, and curtsied.

'Did you see that?' she asked, breaking her own cool demeanour.

'Oh, that was so cool,' said Lisa.

'Come on, quick. Ben, head Mum off before she goes ballistic,' said Tina, as Mum marched across the grass towards them.

Ben raced over to Mum and Lisa watched as her Mum jerked her head, then nodded, then smiled and gave them a friendly waved, all within a heartbeat.

The girls raced over and together they all walked, arm in arm along the path.

The flea man paid them no mind. Finished with his paper, he rose and ambled off.

'How old would you say he is?' asked Tina. 'Fifty, Sixty?'

'No, nowhere near, I'd say mid thirties, maybe forty,' said Mum.

'He looks older,' said Lisa.

'That's because he's bald,' said Mum. 'He's not that old.'

'What else?' said Tina. 'We need more for Daddy.'

'Well,' said Mum. 'He's about six feet tall. I'd say average weight so about fourteen stone, Caucasian...'

'What does that mean?' asked Ben.

'That he's Asian and comes from Ireland,' said Tina.

Mum laughed. 'No, it means he's white. Why Ireland?'

'Oh,' said Tina. 'Cork, Cork is in Ireland. I looked that up. CorkAsian.'

'It's pronounced Cor ca Sian.'

'Cor ca sian,' said Tina. 'Oh yes, that's completely different.'

'Did you see that?' asked Lisa, pointing as the flea man dropped his newspaper into the waste bin. 'We have to get it.'

'Lisa O'Brien, you are not taking stuff out of rubbish bins. Are you listening to me?'

'Sssssshhh,' said Lisa, 'he will hear you. I wasn't thinking of putting *my* hand in there. Gross! But you could.'

'Oh thanks,' said Mum wryly. 'What's so important about an old newspaper, anyway?'

'It might have clues,' said Tina.

'It might have his name,' said Lisa, a flash of inspiration just popping into her head. 'If he has his paper delivered, it would have his name or maybe his address on it.'

'Ummm, actually that is clever thinking.'

As they passed the bin, Mum deftly snagged the newspaper and tucked it under her arm.

Chapter Eighteen

'Let's have a look shall we,' said Mum, as she laid the paper out on the dining table.

Lisa, Tina, and Ben scrambled onto chairs, their eyes scouring the front page for a name or address.

'I can't see anything,' said Tina.

'Maybe it's on the back,' said Mum, flipping the paper over.

Lisa leaned in with everyone else, scanning the newspaper before sitting back disappointed.

'Nothing,' she said.

'Well, don't be downhearted,' said Mum. 'We saw the flea man and can give a pretty good description to Daddy when he gets home.'

'That's true,' said Tina. 'Lisa, what are you doing?'

'Looking up our horoscope,' said Lisa, turning the pages. 'Here we are. Your love life is about to sizzle, and good things are coming your way. Ohhhhh goodie.'

'What good things?' asked Ben. 'What's a love life?'

'A love life is when you have a girlfriend,' said Lisa, 'or in our case a boyfriend. As to what goodies are coming our way?' Lisa thought for a moment. 'The reward. We are going to solve the case and get the rest of the reward money.'

'Now don't go believing in horoscopes,' said Mum, picking up the paper. 'Besides you are too young for boyfriends.'

Lisa and Tina flashed grins at each other before replying in unison, 'Yes, Mum.'

Mum lowered the paper and looked at the girls.

Lisa smiled sweetly as Mum narrowed her eyes at her.

'What?' she said.

'Ummmmmmmm,' Mum said, before going back to reading the paper.

'Come on, let's get our colouring books,' said Lisa.

*

'Oh blast,' said Mum.

'What?' asked Tina, looking up from her colouring book.

'The flea man did the crossword.'

'Oh,' said Tina, returning to her colouring.

'Did he finish it?' asked Lisa pushing herself up from lying on the floor, her colouring book, and pens before her.

'No, there are a few clues left unsolved,' said Mum, biting the top of her pen as she thought. 'If you can't stand the heat, get out of the kitchen. Seven words, starting with P.'

Lisa nibbled the top of pen as she thought. 'Any other letters?'

'Yes, D is the third letter. So P something, D.'

'Pudding,' Lisa said suddenly. 'It's pudding, as in Pudding Lane and the Great Fire of London.'

Tina sat up. 'You mean we actually learnt something useful.'

'Yep,' said Mum. 'You learnt the answer to twenty-five across.'

Mum scribbled the answer down.

'Well done. Let's see how you do with eighteen down. Ready?'

Lisa and Tina both nodded.

'To travel at a moderate pace, especially at sea,' said Mum.

Lisa and Tina turned to each other.

'To travel could be, car, bike, train,' said Lisa.

'But it said *especially* at sea,' said Tina. 'So boat, ship, surfboard.'

'Moderate pace though,' said Lisa. 'So what words describe pace at sea?'

'Steam?' said Tina, looking at Mum.

Mum shook her head. 'Nice idea but it has to start with a C.'

'Oh, you never mentioned that part,' said Tina.

'I thought it might limit your thinking,' said Mum.

'C, C, C,' said Lisa, tapping her lip with her pencil.

'Well, a ship can cut through water.'

Mum shook her head again. 'It has to be six letters.'

'Six! All right, let me think,' said Lisa. 'Powers, no, that's P, clips, nope that's only five letters.'

'Cruise,' said Tina. 'No, that's a type of holiday.'

'Wait,' said Mum. 'Say that again.'

'What, cruise?' said Tina.

'That's it,' said Mum, 'Cruise, yes it can apply to a type holiday, but it also means to travel at a steady pace, and the clue says especially at sea.'

'Yes!' said Tina, high fiving Lisa.

'Good job, girls. Dad will be home soon so I'd best get dinner on.'

Mum went into the kitchen and Lisa turned the paper around so she could have a look at the crossword.

al headwear on the way to the
(3, 3, 2, 5). today can tomorrow
rs who —— up and down (3-3).
ey ——,

DOWN

for a spectacular start (6).
d by our 7 and other Coronation
(5).
ndy luggage (4).
latest choice of dress today (6).
in the cavalcade (8).
ation pageant's pictorial recorder

and 3 (6).
e 2 travellers will listen in (3,
ve officials' mainly pink badge (7)
complete headwear yet there's

123

'Hey look.' she said. 'The local cinema is showing that film we wanted to go and see. Quentin James and the Undercover Agent.'

'Great! We *must* go,' said Tina. 'It was such a great book.'

'I'll say. It was such fun trying to crack the coded messages.'

'Is that the one Daddy read to me?' asked Ben. 'The one about the school for spies?'

'That's the one,' said Tina.

'Can I go?' he asked.

'Let me see. Yes, it's a PG. So, as long as Mum takes us, you're in,' said Lisa.

'Hurray,' said Ben. 'MUM! MUM! Can we go to the cinema, please, please.'

'Hang on,' said Lisa, 'this chap didn't like it. Listen. Whilst the film was full of action, loads of fun and a wonderful feel good movie, the parallels to the first Harry Potter spoilt it for me. 3 stars.'

'What parallels?' said Tina.

'Well, I guess both Quentin and Harry went to a new school. One for spies, the other for magic. They both made friends, Quentin's were Clive, Bluey, and Vicky, whereas Harry's were Ron and Hermione,' said Lisa.

'They both had lessons, Harry was taught magic, and Quentin was taught spycraft.'

'Harry had to fight a troll and a dark wizard,' said Ben.

'Ummmmm Quentin didn't, but he had to figure out who the Undercover Agent was within the school. They both had to take end-of-year exams though,' said Lisa.

'But in the Undercover Agent, we got to see what the exam in spycraft actually was; in Harry Potter they just said they were hard,' said Tina, 'and we could crack the codes in Quentin ourselves, which was the best part, it felt like we were part of the mission.'

'They were not hard for Hermione,' said Ben. 'The exams, I mean.'

'No, she was the clever one,' said Mum, coming out of the kitchen. 'What's all the yelling?'

'Quentin James and the Undercover Agent is on at the cinema. Can we go?'

'Sure. I have never seen you girls so absorbed by a book before, which reminds me, I must check to see if he has written anything else. Now go wash up, dinner will be ready soon.'

Chapter Nineteen

A couple of days later, Lisa, Tina, and Ben were at the dining table having their dinner when Dad walked in.

'Long day?' asked Mum.

Dad nodded.

'Another burglary,' he said, 'at the Fleet's house.'

'Oh no,' said Mum. 'They're on holiday aren't they? What a nightmare to come back too. Was there a lot of damage?'

Dad shook his head.

'No, these are a professional outfit, that's for sure. They only took the high value electrical items such as the TV, DVD player, laptop, and such, some artwork and jewellery.'

'Well that's something at least. Easily replaced and covered by insurance and I'm sure Janice would have taken her best jewellery with her to wear. They're on a cruise aren't they?'

Dad nodded.

'We're debating whether to send a message to the ship and tell them or wait until they get home.'

'Why not send a car to meet them when they land and tell them then? I suspect they will fly back from their last port of call. That way you can offer them a ride home and be there when they enter their home. I am sure they will appreciate that.'

Dad gathered Mum into his arms and gave her a kiss.

'I married such a clever wife,' he said.

'Any clues?' asked Tina.

Dad shook his head. 'Even our usual suspects have alibis. For instance, Jack Jackson would be a firm favorite to be involved but last night he says he was at the cinema, watching that Quentin movie you kids want to go and see.'

Mum snorted. 'Like you don't.'

'Well, I am happy to spend time with my lovely family and if they wish to go and see a kid's film, then I am willing to go along too.'

'Pull the other one,' said Mum. 'You read that book to Ben every night and loved every minute of it.'

'It was so good,' said Dad. 'I never guessed who the spy was, though the clues were right there.'

'Did he like it? The movie I mean,' asked Lisa.

Dad shook his head.

'Actually, no, he said the parallels to Harry Potter spoilt it for him, though it was a fun, feel good movie, and action packed.'

'That's just what the man in the paper said,' said Tina.

'What was that?' asked Dad.

'That suspect, Jack Jackson, he said exactly what the critic said in the paper,' said Lisa.

Dad got up and paced. 'He had a ticket, but that doesn't mean he saw the movie. Moreover, if he read the paper he would have seen the review. Very good, very good indeed.'

'Still want to go and see it?' asked Mum.

'Er?' said Dad.

'The movie, do you still want to go and see it, given the review and all?'

Lisa held her breath. She could see the twinkle in Mum's eye so knew she was teasing Dad, but if Dad said no, Mum would probably suggest waiting for the DVD and that was ages away.

'Absolutely. I can draw parallels to Harry Potter in many TV shows, movies, books and vice versa, doesn't mean it's a bad book or going to be a bad movie. I'm looking forward to it. We'll go Friday night. Have a pizza beforehand.'

Lisa jumped up and down cheering, along with Ben and Tina.

'We're going to the cinema and having a pizza as well. YIPPPEEEEEEEE!'

Later in bed, Lisa was thinking about the burglaries.

'There's something bugging me about the Fleet's robbery,' said Lisa. 'But I cannot put my finger on it.'

'I know,' said Tina. 'I was thinking the same thing. Something about the cruise.'

'Yes, something we've seen on TV do you think?'

'Must have been, a detective show, Castle perhaps? Or Bones?'

Lisa screwed her nose up. 'I hope it's not Bones,' she said. 'We might find a dead body or something.'

'Oh that would be great. It would be all gooey and grisly,' said Tina with relish. 'They're always like that.'

'Ewwww, you would throw up if you saw one,' said Lisa. 'You know you would.'

'Maybe,' said Tina. 'But can you imagine Show and Tell in school? That would be so cool.'

'Be nice to go on a cruise,' said Lisa.

'Be nice to go on holiday,' said Tina.

'That's it!' said Lisa, sitting up.

Chapter Twenty

'Night, kiddo,' said Dad.

'Night, Dad,' said Ben.

Dad switched off the bedside lamp and closed the door.

'Dad?'

'Yes, son?'

'Can you leave the light on?'

Dad slipped back into the room and sat on Ben's bed.

'It's been a while since you slept with the light on Ben. What's up?'

'We might get burgled. The burglars are robbing houses now.'

'Arrr, I see,' said Dad. 'Come on, let me show you something.'

Dad scooped Ben up from his bed and carried him out onto the landing.

'Lisa, what are you doing out of bed?'

'I thought of something,' she said. 'About the robberies.'

'Ok, give me a minute with Ben then I'll come in and see you, ok?'

'Mind if I come too?'

'You heard?'

Lisa nodded.

Lisa followed Dad and Ben down the stairs.

'See all those locks?' said Dad. 'They will keep out any burglar. And,' he added, 'see here, all the windows have locks on them too.'

Dad gave the handle a shake to show it was secure. 'And to top all of that,' he said, tapping the box fixed on the wall. 'We have a security alarm system fitted.'

Ben had looked at the door, and then over at the windows before studying the alarm system box carefully before nodding.

'They're not getting in are they, Daddy.'

Dad shook his head. 'No, son, they are not getting in here.'

'We should get a dog though, to protect the house,' Ben added.

Dad laughed. 'You and dogs. Maybe when you're older.'

Dad took Ben back upstairs and tucked him into bed.

'You can have the light on if you like,' he said.

Ben shook his head, yawning.

'Good boy,' said Dad, ruffling his hair.

Closing the door quietly, Ben's eyes already closed, Dad turned around to Lisa.

'Back to bed,' he said quietly.

Lisa led the way back to her bedroom and jumped into bed as Dad pulled up the quilt around her.

'Now, you were saying you thought of something.'

'Yes,' said Lisa. 'The other robberies, were the owners on holiday as well?'

Lisa watched her Dad closely, hoping for what he called a "light bulb" moment but she was disappointed when he shrugged.

'I'm not sure, why?'

'Oh, it's probably nothing. Tina and I remembered seeing something on TV once where people on holiday were being robbed. I thought it might be a clue.'

'It might be,' said Dad. 'It just might be. Leave it with me. I'll check back on the other cases in the morning.'

Lisa beamed and snuggled down under her quilt.

'Go to sleep now,' said Dad, kissing Lisa on the forehead.

'Night, Dad,' said Tina.

'Night, girls.'

Chapter Twenty One

'Tina, Lisa,' said Ben, bursting into their room. 'Dad's home and he's got news.'

Lisa leapt up and just beat Tina to the door. Ben was already dashing down the stairs.

'Wait, wait, wait,' cried Tina, her feet pounding on the stairs as she rushed down.

'No running!' yelled Dad.

'Yes, Dad,' Lisa called back, stopping herself in front of the lounge door and walking in calmly.

'If everyone is seated comfortably,' said Dad, looking around the group. 'Lisa, your idea about the burglaries being related to the victims being on holiday, was an excellent one. Whilst not every house or shop owner was on holiday, they were all away for some reason or another.'

'So the burglars knew the house or shop would be vacant?' said Lisa. 'That's the right word, vacant?'

'Yes, that's the right word. Question is how did they know? I was hoping you remembered more of that TV program you saw, Lisa.'

Lisa shook her head.

'That's okay,' said Dad. 'It might come to you later. So, anyway, the Fleet's returned from their cruise today, and we ran them home.'

'They live over on Duke Street, right?' said Mum. 'Have there been any other burglaries in that street?'

Dad shook his head.

'Hang on!' said Lisa, jumping up in excitement.

She rushed out of the room and up the stairs, grabbed the flea man's newspaper, and charged back down.

'Here,' she said breathlessly.

Spreading out the paper, she stabbed her finger down onto the crossword.

The crossword grid contains the following filled-in answers:

FORTY-SECOND
BABBLER / MARUM
ABRA / EVENING
FAT
FAULT / PETTY
SATURDAY / FOR
DOUCE
TRAN / OKE
PUDDING / EXTRE

Left margin clue fragments:
...ing / ...her / ...our / ...l. 3.

...of / ...h o / ...pro- / ...lear-

...s not / Coro- / one's / ...(4). / ...n of / ...the / ...l re- / . / ...ondon / l o n e / ...ondon / ...y (5), / ...e g e d / ...pecta-

...r eme / ...l a tion / ...7). / ...s pro- / ...memo- / ...(5).

...al headwear on the way to the
(3, 3, 2, 5),
...rs who —— today can tomorrow
...ey ——, up and down (3-3).

DOWN
...for a spectacular start (6).
...d by our 7 and other Coronation
...(5).
...ndy luggage (4).
...s latest choice of dress today (6).
...s in the cavalcade (8).
...ation pageant's pictorial recorder
...i and 3 (6).
...e 2 travellers will listen in (3,
...ve officials' mainly pink badge (7).
...omplete headwear yet there's

SOLUTION TO No. 3,321

THE SIGN OF FOU(R)
H G N O L
R RUFUS EXTR
E E E I E
ENTERED TRAM
A D E R
NAMELY ARMAD
D A I H
TITAN ANTONI
H E C G E
RODEO GOTHS
E L A A T
ESSENTIAL FAT

...don't over crow

'Look at the answers; Cruise, Fleet, and Duke, there's even a Street, a Five, a Saturday, and an Evening. It's all here.'

Dad moved the paper around so he could read it properly.

'I bet the Fleet's lived at Number Five Duke's Street and were robbed Saturday Evening,' said Lisa.

'Well?' asked Mum.

Dad nodded. 'Spot on. Lisa, my girl, you've cracked it!'

Lisa squealed as Dad picked her up and spun her around.

'It was all of us really,' said Lisa, when Dad finally put her down.

'Tina and Mum helped with the crossword and Ben helped too.'

'You are all first rate detectives,' said Dad. 'I am so proud of you all.'

Lisa beamed and knew Tina and Ben were every bit as proud and happy as she was.

Chapter Twenty Two

The following afternoon.

'Girls, can you deliver these letters for me?'

'Sure, Mum,' said Tina.

Lisa and Tina put on their shoes and walked together along the street, popping through the gate of the houses Mum had addressed envelopes too, and posting the letters through their letterbox.

'Here's Mr Willow's place,' said Lisa, opening the gate.

'Wait, wait,' said Tina, looking through the letters, 'There's not one for Mr Willow this time.'

'That's odd, he usually gets a letter.'

'Maybe Mum forgot.'

'Must have. Come on. Let's post the last of these and ran back so Mum can print off another copy.'

Posting the last letter they rushed back home.

'Mum, Mum' cried Lisa, racing into the kitchen. 'You forgot about Mr Willow, there was no letter for him.'

'I hadn't forgotten, he's on holiday.'

Lisa took a sharp intake of breath.

'What if he's next to be burgled?'

'That's how the burglars know who is going to be away from their home,' said Tina.

'What do you mean?' asked Mum.

'What if they're cancelling their newspaper delivery?'

'That's genius,' said Lisa.

Mum nodded thoughtfully.

'It is and I think worth calling your Dad right away.'

Lisa and Tina hugged each other as they stood with Mum in the hallway as she dialled the police station.

*

'Dad's very impressed with you girls,' said Mum, putting down the phone.

'You were right, according to yesterday's crossword, Mr Willow's house is going to be burgled tonight, and Dad will be waiting to catch them in the act. Figuring out the cancellation of the newspaper delivery was the last piece of the puzzle.'

'Can we be there?' asked Tina. 'When they catch them.'

'Absolutely not,' said Mum.

Tina pouted but didn't argue, and Lisa knew she hadn't really expected to be allowed, but it's always worth asking.

*

Lisa woke in the middle of the night to the sounds of soft conversation and she tiptoed to the door and opened it, just a little.

'We arrested them all.'

'So the case is closed?'

'Yep, the mastermind behind the gang worked for the paper. He knew whenever anyone cancelled their paper delivery and had a crossword published to alert the others.'

'And the girls cracked it,' said Mum.

'They did indeed. Every shop owner has agreed to honour their reward, especially as they all got their stolen items back. The gang were sitting on the lot, keeping it in a warehouse on the edge of town. In that industrial park, you know?'

'We'll take the girls into town on Saturday and open that bank account,' said Mum.

'Ben too,' said Dad.

'Ben too,' agreed Mum.

Lisa closed the door quietly and tiptoed back to bed, thoughts of all the shades of lipstick she could buy sending her off to sleep.

THE
O'BRIEN
DETECTIVE
AGENCY
~~No~~ BROTHERS
~~aLOUD~~
allowed

THE END

THE LIBRARY

1

JEFFERSON HIGH SCHOOL

DANVILLE

Virginia

The United States of America

Alex looked up at the sign then back down the long path to where his Mum stood.

She waved, and he waved back, feeling his eyes prick.

Get a grip, he thought.

He took a deep breath and stepped into the school building, the cool air instantly noticeable to the summer heat outside.

I didn't cough. Maybe the warm air is good for me here.

"Hello young man, you must be Alex Powell? I'm Mr Cisco, the Principal. Come along. I'll show you around and then introduce you to your classmates."

Alex shook the Principal's hand and followed him around the school, nodding his head at the appropriate moments.

The school looked great, nothing like the huge inner city monoliths, with their metal detectors, high wire fencing,

147

and grim exteriors he had expected from the movies. No, the school in Danville was bright and modern, and he was looking forward to next term, after hearing all about the challenging programs and after school clubs on offer. All of them looked great, though he was a little disappointed to find the Forensic Club didn't attend murder scenes, solve crimes and examine bodies but engaged in a variety of debates geared towards public speaking, which didn't sound very CSI to him at all.

"I think it was a very good idea of yours to come in this afternoon, get the lay of the land so to speak. Ah, here we are, this is your classroom," said Mr Cisco, opening the door.

Alex walked in, looking across at all the kids in the class, blushing under their scrutiny, as several comments were clearly audible.

"Who's that?"

"Beats me."

"QUIET!" barked the teacher.

"Sssshhh."

"You ssssshh."

"Would you both SSSSSHHHH! It may be the last day of term but I will not have talking in my classroom, is that understood, Katie? Chip?"

"Yeh, sorry," said Katie, glaring at Chip.

Chip grinned back, which made Alex smile.

"Welcome, Alex, right? Welcome to the class. My name is Mr Edwards, your History Teacher."

Alex shook the offered hand.

"Class, Alex is from England and will be joining us next term. Alex, why don't you take that desk over there."

Alex nodded and moved to the empty desk, placing his backpack on top. He winced as the chair legs scrapped noisily in the quiet of the classroom and sat down with a bump, to a few giggles.

"Ok, class; let's get back to the lesson."

*

Katie looked over at the new boy, her mind abuzz with curiosity.

A tap on her shoulder alerted her to a note about to be passed.

Hand down low; Katie reached as far back as she could until the paper was pressed into her palm.

Slowly, keeping her face intent on the board, she brought her hand up and onto her lap.

With several loud coughs, she unfolded the paper and spread it out on her lap.

"Are you ok, Katie?"

"Yes, fine, thank you."

Casting her eyes downwards, she read the note.

That must be him

Her fingers crawled over the desk, like a large spider, to her pen before she slipped the note onto her desk and scribbled on the paper. She folded it and dropping her hand low, passed it backwards.

That must be him

Yes, but who is he?

Within a minute, there was a tap on her shoulder and the note was once again in her lap.

That must be him

Yes, but who is he?

The New Boy.

Katie let out an exaggerated sigh. Of course he was the new boy, that was obvious, but *who* was he and why was he here on the *last* day of term?

"Katie?"

"Yes?"

"Are you paying attention?"

"Yes, Mr Edwards."

"What was the year the Civil War ended?"

Kate looked at the board only to find Mr Edwards had covered the date with his hand.

"1865."

Mr Edwards looked at her intently for a moment.

"Ummmpf, yes, correct," he said, turning back to the board.

Her friends in the front row took their hands from behind their backs, each having shown one number with their fingers.

Katie looked across to her best friend in the whole world, Lucy, shrugged her shoulders, and pointed to the young man sitting at the front of the class.

Lucy shrugged her shoulders in return and looked towards the back of the class where Chuck was sitting.

Chuck pointed at the new boy before lifting one arm, and dropping his head to one side, as if hung.

"Chuck! Are you having a fit?" asked Mr Edwards, eliciting chuckles around the classroom. "No? Then please refrain from the pantomime performance, and Katie, unless you want detention I suggest you turn around and PAY ATTENTION!"

"Yes, Mr Edwards."

A trickle of fear tingled down Katie's back. Mr Edwards was the only teacher in the whole wide world who would give out detention on the *last* day of school! He was the only one giving an *actual* lesson. The noise of games and laughter filtered down the corridor and through the door to torture them as they sat and listened to facts about the Civil War. BORRRRING!

Katie jumped as another tap on her shoulder startled her from her thoughts. She reached backwards to retrieve the note.

He's the boy who moved into Black House!

We'll get him after school

That was as far as she got before the paper was snatched from her hand, tearing as it was pulled from her fingers.

"So what have we got here?" said Mr Edwards.

He walked to the front of the class, balling the note within his fist, his hand shaking with anger.

BANG!

Everyone jumped in their chairs, silence descended on the room, no one dared move, dared breathe for fear of drawing the teacher's attention on them.

"I will not abide bullying! Is that Clear?"

All the boys and girls looked at each other.

"IS THAT CLEAR?"

"Yes," said Lucy, her voice faltering.

"Yes, Mr Edwards!" chorused the rest of the classroom.

"Alex!" Mr Edwards snapped.

Alex jumped in his seat.

"Yes, Sir?" said Alex.

"I hope you have enjoyed your day at school and I look forward to seeing you in my classroom next term."

"Thank you, Sir."

"It is tradition here that a new boy or girl gets to leave a little earlier than the rest, so pack up your things and be off with you."

"Yes, Sir," said Alex.

Katie looked at Lucy who shrugged. She had never heard of that tradition before.

"Straight home, my boy, straight home you hear?"

*

Alex looked at Mr Edwards and nodded, a wave of sadness flowing over him as he walked across the room to the door.

"Go on lad, the last bell will sound soon."

"Yes, Mr Edwards."

Alex opened the door and stepped into the corridor, his heart sinking. The day hadn't gone as he had hoped.

Shouldering his backpack, he jogged down the corridor towards the main entrance. He didn't know what was on the piece of paper, but Mr Edwards was clearly warning him.

Alex stepped into the bright sunlight of the afternoon, the last bell sounded behind him. Alex looked over his shoulder as the kids poured out of their classrooms, shouting and larking about, enjoying the moment that heralded the start of the summer holidays.

He took off at a run.

Back in Mr Edward's classroom, the boys and girls still sat as Mr Edwards paced up and down. All eyes on the clock as the second hand ticked away.

"Okay, you may leave. Enjoy your holidays and I will see you all next term."

Katie only heard "Okay" before she was pushing her chair back, grabbing her bag, and joining the throng of kids as they pushed and shoved to get out of the door. She glanced again at the scrap of paper she still held within her palm.

WE MUST WARN HIM!

*

The Library

OUT NOW

Available on Kindle and Paperback

© 2017 Simon Hartwell

This book is a work of fiction. All characters in the publication are fictitious and any resemblances to real persons, living or dead are purely coincidental.

Contact

http://simonhartwell.blogspot.co.uk/

simonhartwell @rocketmail.com

32102390R00090

Printed in Poland
by Amazon Fulfillment
Poland Sp. z o.o., Wrocław